Frankenstein's Dog

story by Jan Wahl
pictures by Kay Chorao

Prentice-Hall, Inc., Englewood Cliffs, New Jersey

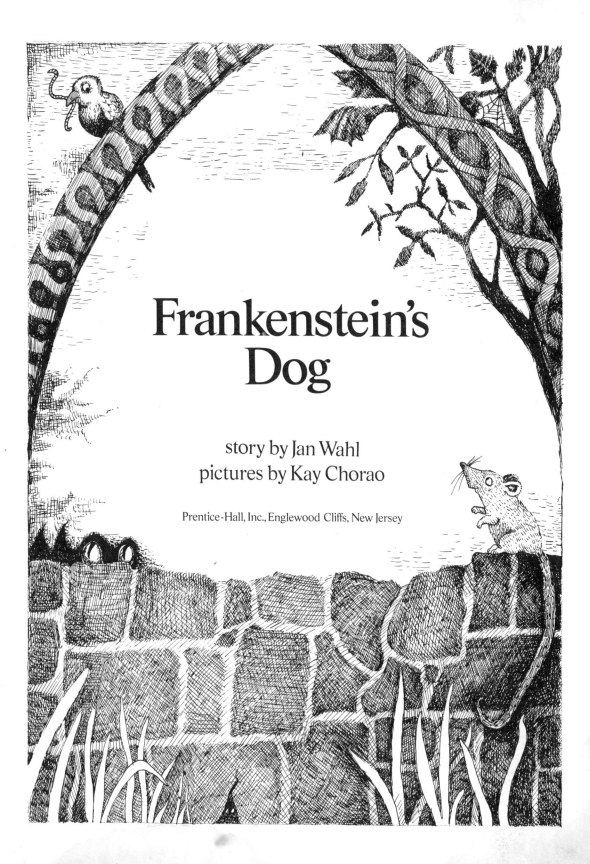

Frankenstein's Dog

story by Jan Wahl
pictures by Kay Chorao

Prentice-Hall, Inc., Englewood Cliffs, New Jersey

Printed in the United States of America   •J

Prentice-Hall International, Inc., London
Prentice-Hall of Australia, Pty. Ltd., North Sydney
Prentice-Hall of Canada, Ltd., Toronto
Prentice-Hall of India Private Ltd., New Delhi
Prentice-Hall of Japan, Inc., Tokyo
Prentice-Hall of Southeast Asia Pte. Ltd., Singapore

10 9 8 7 6 5 4 3 2 1

Library of Congress Cataloging in Publication Data

Wahl, Jan.
   Frankenstein's dog.

   SUMMARY: A dog's eye view of his master and his master's monster.
   [1. Dogs—Fiction.   2. Monsters—Fiction]   I. Chorao, Kay.   II. Title.
   PZ7.W1266Fr   [E]   77-3674
   ISBN 0-13-330522-8

To Andy

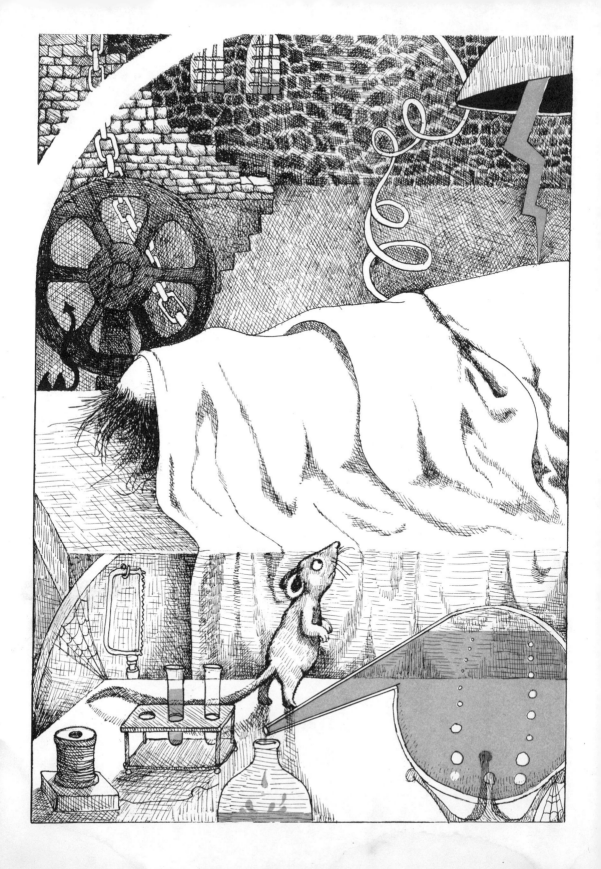

My master, Doctor Frankenstein, is building a man thing.

They call it The Monster. *It looks* nice enough to me. Though I am just a dog. Frankenstein's dog. "AARRFFF!"

Doctor Frankenstein is showing Monster how to walk. It is hard for him. Two days old. Watch him walk . . . Any puppy can do better than that! Look at me!

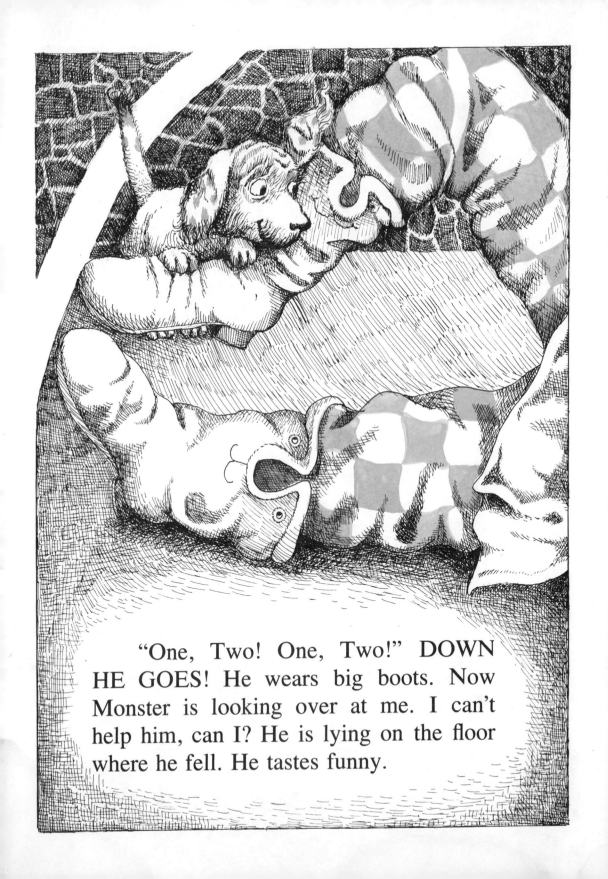

"One, Two! One, Two!" DOWN
HE GOES! He wears big boots. Now
Monster is looking over at me. I can't
help him, can I? He is lying on the floor
where he fell. He tastes funny.

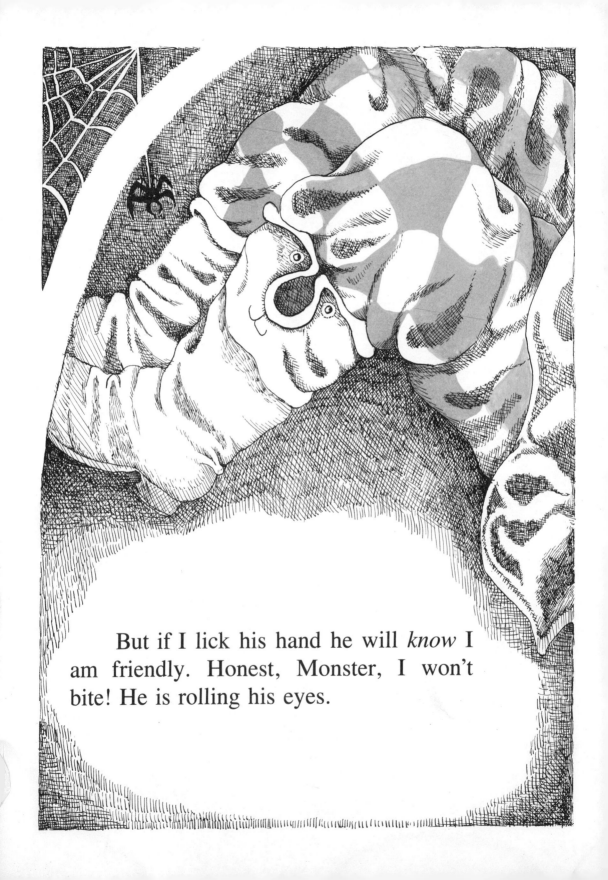

But if I lick his hand he will *know* I am friendly. Honest, Monster, I won't bite! He is rolling his eyes.

Doctor Frankenstein and his helper, Schnickelfritz, put poor Monster back on his feet again. Good luck!

"One, Two! One, Two!" Do your stuff, Mister Monster. Outside the birds are singing. Monster waves at them and wants to listen. He is trying to sing, also.

The yellow sun is too shiny for his new eyes. He blinks. I guide him by taking his pants in my teeth. Slowly.

Doctor Frankenstein throws me a stick. Stupid game! I am to bring it back. All right. I bring it back. Now he throws it again! How dumb does he think I am?

Guess what? This time Monster wants to fetch the stick. This game is growing better! He is learning to walk. So we try to see who gets it first. Monster or me.

At last Frankenstein and Schnickel-fritz let us alone. I show Monster where I hide bones. He helps me dig. I show him my favorites. He is bigger. He takes the most. He is smart for a monster.

Now it is supper-time. We each have
a bowl on the floor. Yuck. Mush again—
with paprika. *He* seems to love it!

"Monster," I try to suggest. "Let us be *good* friends." He grunts in a strange way. We tussle. He understands.

It is time to sleep. Together we stretch out on the hard floor. Monster and me. Dear Monster, Good Night! SLEEP TIGHT, DON'T LET THE BED BUGS BITE!